KB139304

영원한 교향곡 0번
Eternal Symphony No,0

최경희

한국문학세상

시는 문학과 예술의 통합점으로 사람의 내면은 어디에서나 빛나고 다양하고 다채로운 눈물을 담고 있는 예술이라고 생각합니다.

삶은 절망과 깊은 고민을 극복한 여정으로 깨달음과 명료함을 얻게 되며 시련과 고난을 겪으면서 기쁨과 슬픔의 다채로움을 깨달으며 집중하는 중요성을 알게 됩니다.

그런 영적 깨달음과 깊은 감성을 담은 「영원한 교향곡 0번_Eternal Symphony No. 0」은 다양한 독자를 만나기 위해 한글과 영문을 동시에 게재한 이중언어 시집입니다.

이 시집은 영적 성장과 깨달음의 순간들을 담고 있으며, 시를 통해 내면의 평화와 향기, 주변의 아름다움에 대한 깊은 사색을 느끼게 해 줍니다.

시는 그림 같은 풍경과 감동적인 감정 그리고 생명의 신비로움을 담았습니다.

독자들은 이중언어 시집을 읽으면서 소중한 순간을 선물하고 새로운 시각과 통찰력을 제공하여 영혼의 여정을 함께

나누는 공감의 원천을 만끽하게 될 것 같습니다.

　또한 이 시집은 한국어로 쓴 제 시를 영어로 다시 쓴 이중 언어 시집입니다. 하지만 시를 영어로 표현하면서 저만의 관점이 깊게 들어갔기 때문에 직역하면 또 다른 느낌이 전달될 수도 있습니다. 시의 특성을 고려하셔서 읽어주시기 바랍니다.

　마지막으로 저의 시집이 세상 밖으로 나올 수 있도록 출간의 길을 열어 준 「한국문학세상」 관계자와 격려를 아끼지 않았던 모든 분에게 감사드립니다.

저자 최경희 드림

I believe that poetry is the integration of literature and art, and is an art that shines everywhere inside a person and contains diverse and colorful tears.

Life is a journey of overcoming despair and deep anxiety, gaining enlightenment and clarity, and through trials and tribulations, we realize the variety of joys and sorrows and learn the importance of focus.

「Eternal Symphony No. 0」 contains such spiritual enlightenment and deep emotions. 0" is a bilingual poetry book published simultaneously in Korean and English to reach a variety of readers.

This book of poems contains moments of spiritual growth and enlightenment, and through the poetry, it allows you to feel inner peace, scent, and deep contemplation of the beauty around you.

The poem contains picturesque landscapes, touching emotions, and the mystery of life.

By reading this bilingual poetry book, readers will enjoy

a source of empathy that presents precious moments, provides new perspectives and insights, and shares the soul's journey.

This poetry book is a bilingual book of poems written in Korean, rewritten in English. However, because I put my own perspective deeply into the poem while expressing it in English, a literal translation may convey a different feeling. Please read while considering the characteristics of the poem.

Lastly, I would like to thank the staff of "Korean Literary World" for opening the way for my poetry book to be published and all those encouraged me.

Author Kyunghee Choi

제2부

제3부

제1부

그리움 Longing

그리움 맺혀 흐르는 눈물들은
서글픈 기억과 함께 흘러가네
저 하늘에 떠오르는 달빛 같은
그리운 이의 얼굴 보이누나

옛날 추억의 소중한 품에 안긴
따스한 향기로 함께 떠오르는
내 마음이 그리움 파도를 따라
가슴 깊이 멍울져 시작된 눈물

때론 쓰리고 아린 눈물들이
가슴 휘젓기를 반복하지만
때론 움푹 패인 낭자함들을
기억하고 힘을 주기도 해

그리움 맺혀 흐르는 눈물들이
흐르는 시간만큼 더 깊어지고
흐르는 강처럼 흐르는 노래로
수채화빛 유화로 벽에 걸렸다

Longing 그리움

The tears of longing
Sad memories flow
Like moonlight in the sky,
I see the face of the one I miss.

Longing for the old memory,
Rising with a warm scent
My heart follows the waves of longing
Tears that started deep in my haert.

Sometimes those bitter, painful tears
Shake the heart repeatedly,
but sometimes they remind us of the pains
and give me strength.

Tears of longing
deepen with time
and become a song like a flowing river.
Hanging on the wall as an oil painting in watercolor colors.

나의 우주 My universe

이른 새벽 하늘을 보며
빛나는 별들 눈에 담아
눈 감고도 헤아린다
그 별이 아직 그 자리에 있다
지금처럼 그리 있었다
더 빛나기 위해
가슴 한껏 팽창하여 터지는
밤별과 새벽별들도
여전히 빛나고 있다
그때처럼 어슴프레한 그곳 밝히려
스스로 끌어안고 터지며
억겁의 시간과 정지된 시간 속에
그리 존재해 왔던가
내 가슴에도 별들 품은 우주 있었다

My universe 나의 우주

While gazing at the early dawn sky,

I capture each and every shining star with my eyes.

Even with closed eyes, I count the stars I can see.

Those stars are still in their places,

Just as they were before, right now.

To shine even brighter,

The night stars and dawn stars expand to their fullest and burst,

Yet they still continue to shine. Just like back then.

In order to illuminate that faint place,

I embrace it myself and burst,

Have I existed within the vastness of time or frozen time?

In my heart, there was also a universe

That embraced the stars.

빛의 위로 The light's consolation

봄에는 새싹 향기 품은 햇살 될게요
당신의 꿈과 희망 사라지지 않도록

여름에는 숲 향기 진한 햇볕 될게요
당신이 가는 길에 열정빛 머물도록

가을에는 청아한 푸른 하늘 될게요
당신의 보금자리에 온기 머물도록

겨울에는 순백빛 눈꽃 향수 될게요
당신의 마음 그 자리 정결해지도록

제일 높은 곳에서 빛 될게요

The light's consolation 빛의 위로

In spring, I will become the sunlight with the fragrance of
sprouting plants,
So that your dreams and hopes never fade away.

In summer, I will become the strong sunlight with the
scent of the forest,
So that passion shines upon the path you walk.

In autumn, I will become the clear blue sky,
So that warmth dwells in your sanctuary.

In winter, I will become the fragrance of pure white snow-
flakes,
So that your heart becomes pure and beautiful.

At the highest place, I will become the light.

우주가 된 조각들 Pieces that became a universe

내 안에서 유영하던 조각들아
서로 다른 모습으로 내재하던 너희들
거울도 필요 없이 하나로

각기 다른 색상과 형태 가진 조각들
날카로운 가시 부드러운 꽃잎으로
모두 하나의 동그라미 되어가고.

그물에 얽혔던 불안과 혼돈의 파편들
조금씩 깍이고 연마된 매끄러운 빛결
이 얼마나 아름다운 균형인가

무수한 참빛과 반대의 조각들
모든 것은 하나의 원되어
에너지 발원지의 복원이랄까

조각들이 하늘되고 우주되어
더는 분리되지 않는 오묘한 날갯짓으로
완전함의 시식 공간될려나

Pieces that became a universe 우주가 된 조각들

Pieces that used to float within me
Were inherent in different forms
One state without mirrors

Pieces with different colors and shapes
Sharp thorns are becoming soft petals...
All becoming one circle.

Fragments of anxiety and chaos tangled in a net
Little by little, polished and polished to a smooth shine.
What a beautiful balance.

Countless shards of true light and its opposites,
Everything became a circle
Has the Energy Center recovered

The fragments become heavenly and cosmic
No longer separated, but fluttering in exquisite wings.
Is it going to be a perfect tasting place

물의 미학 Aesthetics of water

물은 흐르면서 어디든지 자유하며
피하고 부딪히고 스며들고 낙하하면서
최적의 세공된 보석 남긴다

물은 고이면서 그 어디에 걸림없이
스미고 쓸어내고 씻어주고 희석되면서
많은 부유물과 침전물 남긴다

물은 지나가며 그 어디에 고착없이
뜨겁고 식혀주고 얼려주고 해빙되면서
잊거나 찾거나 잃은 기억 남긴다

물은 살리면서 그 어디에 머뭄없이
마르고 넘쳐나며 빈곤과 풍요를 주면서
때로 모든 생명들 향한 교훈 남긴다

Aesthetics of water 물의 미학

Water flows, free to go wherever it pleases
Dodging, bumping, soaking, and falling
leaving behind optimally crafted jewelry

The water stagnates, but it doesn't get stuck anywhere.
It smears, sweeps, washes, dilutes.
leaving behind many floats and sediments.

The water passes by, leaving nothing behind.
As it heats, cools, freezes, thaws.
leaving memories to be forgotten, found, or lost

Water is life, and doesn't stay.
Drying up and overflowing, giving poverty and abundance.
Sometimes leaving lessons for all life.

통증은 또 다른 꽃이 되어 피고

Pain becomes another flower and blooms

바람이 불었다
산에는 나무가 부러졌고
바다에는 높은 파도 쳐댔다

이 나이 되어서야 알게 된 삶은
많이 아프고 때로는 슬프고
한없는 고통의 나락으로 떨어져
더는 떨어질 곳 없어 바닥이 패이기도 했다

그 끝에 외로움이라는 막다른 골목
절망이 희망으로 감아오를 때까지
아무것도 할 수 없다는 걸 확인하고
돌아서고 싶지만 돌아갈 수 없다

그래 이제는 가벼워져
떠오르거나 날아가는 것만이
푸른 숲 볼 수 있는 게다

힘을 놓아 버려
뼈 마디 혈관까지 무력해지도록
그것만이 날아오를 날개 만드는 방법이야

Pain becomes another flower and blooms

통증은 또 다른 꽃이 되어 피고

The wind blew

broke trees in the mountains

and the sea crashed with high waves.

At this age life, as I have come to know it.

It hurts a lot, sometimes sad

I fell into a spiral of endless pain

There was no place to fall anymore, and I hit rock bottom.

A dead end of loneliness at the end of it all

Until despair turns into hope

I see that I can't do anything

I want to turn around, but I can't go back

So now I feel lighter

Only floating or flying

I can see the green forest

Let go of your strength

Every bone in your body, every blood vessel is powerless.

That's the only way to build wings to fly.

마구니들의 합창 이후 흔적

A trace of the day when the demons sang together

청아한 겨울 날 새벽빛이 햇살 만날 때

스스로 지혜롭다 여긴 착각의 방종

거기만의 틀 안에 끼우려 물길 틀었다 한다
그것은 가장 어둡고 멋없는 흑색 뿌리였으므로

어느 한 쪽은 가뭄이고
어느 한 쪽은 홍수만 낭자했더랬지

A trace of the day
when the demons sang together

마구니들의 합창 이후 흔적

When the first rays of dawn meet the sun on a clear winter day.

A certain indulgence that thought itself wise

It bent the water to fit into its own mold.
It was the darkest and most ungainly of black roots.

One side is dry and thirsty,
and One was humid and foggy.

이목과 소홀 사이 Between focus and neglect

아무것도 아닌 것 붙잡지 마
그 바닥으로 간 건 디딤돌 찾은 거야
나를 버리고 다 타 버리면 아무것도 아닌 것을

Between focus and neglect 이목과 소홀 사이

Don't hold on to something that's nothing.

Getting lost and falling into traps can be a stepping-stone.

If myself abandon myself and burn out, nothing more

일관성의 환상 (부제: 갇힌 그림자)

Ilusions of Uniformity (Subtitle: Trapped shadow)

다름을 인정해 주니
자기와 똑같다라고
검은색을 희다라고
하얀색을 검다라고
착각의 안경을 끼고
같아 달라 우기더라

편향되고 갇힌 것도
흘러가다 희석되면
검은 것도 회색이고
하얀 것도 회색이고
연한 것과 진한 것의
단조로운 합창일 뿐

찬 달빛아래 솟아난
삐죽한 끄트머리의
가슴 속 잿빛 멍울만
굳어진 채 설기설기
찰그락대며 떨어진
달빛 조각이 춤춘다

Illusions of Uniformity
(Subtitle: Trapped shadow)

일관성의 환상 (부제: 갇힌 그림자)

When acknowledging differences,

They mistook themselves as identical,

Seeing black as white,

And white as black,

Wearing the glasses of delusion,

Insisting on being the same.

Even when biases and confinement

Flow and dilute over time,

Black turns into shades of gray,

And white also turns into shades of gray,

The light and dark tones of the

It's just a monotonous chorus

Under the chilly moonlight,

From the jagged edges of tangled thoughts,

Only the ash-colored lump in the heart

Remains frozen, softly,

With a clattering sound,

Moonlit fragments dance.

미스테리 통증 **Mystery Soreness**

뿌리마저 희미하지만 좀 아프더라
너도 아프니? 나는 조금 더 아프더라
아무것도 모르는데 왜 아직 아플까

Mystery Soreness 미스테리 통증

Even though the roots are faint, it still heartbreaking a bit.

Are you heartbreaking too? I'm heartbreaking a little more.

Why am I still in pain when I know nothing?

무지개빛 꽃 Iridescent Blossoms

만개한 한 송이 꽃도
떨어져 시든 꽃잎도
한 때는 모두 점이었다

피고 지는 것이 꽃이듯
어느 꽃인들 비 안 맞고
피고 질 수 없는 게야

빨주노초파남보 꽃이
피고 지고 거듭되는 건
모든 사람들 이치야

Iridescent Blossoms 무지개빛 꽃

A single Blossoms in full bloom,
Falling petals that wither soon,
Once they were all mere dots.

Flowers bloom and fade.
All flowers need rain or they will die.
without rain....

Red, orange, yellow, green, blue, indigo, and violet flowers
blooming and fading is
everyone's way.

바머팅 Vomiting

강하거나
진하거나
매콤하고
찡하거나
습하거나
칼칼하고
알싸리한
'말'이 뱉어질 때는
다 이유가 있는 것

Vomiting 바머팅

Strong or

thick or

spicy

sour

humid

sharp

Nausea and other

When 'words' are spit out

They all happen for a reason.

장막 너머 **Beyond the Veil**

끊임없이 흐르고 돌며
망부석처럼 머무르지

염증이 가시처럼 찔러
무감각 일상에 물들고

불변의 법칙 그 어딘가
안주의 커튼 드리워진

저 안개 너머 내딛고저

Beyond the Veil 장막 너머

Flowing and turning incessantly
Like a rock that can't move

Subtle pain that feels like inflammation
The dull routine continues

Somewhere amidst the immutable laws
The curtain of complacency is drawn

I step beyond that mist

망각의 영역 In the Realm of Oblivion

망각의 파도 속 상흔은
아득히 멀어져 간다지만
기억의 미로 속에 머무르고

잊었다, 억지스레 긁어내듯
닿을 수 없게 방치해야만 해
그림자 겹친 거기에 있어

고된 망각의 꽃 만개하면
그 순간 흔들린 틈 사이로
광챗빛 닮은 휘장 두르고

기억의 그곳에서
망각의 실타래와 새 텃빛
공존의 왈츠 잔치 열리지

In the Realm of Oblivion 망각의 영역

It is said that in the waves of oblivion, the scars

It's said they fade away

I stay in the maze of memories

Forgot, as if forcibly scraping it away.

I must leave it untouchable.

There in the shadows

When the laborious flower of forgetfulness is in full bloom.

Through the chasms that shook at that moment

Wearing a sash that resembles a ray of light.

In a Place of Memory

Threads of Oblivion and a new light of area.

The Waltz of Coexistence is celebrated

고요함의 역설 The Paradox of Stillness

가끔은 생각에 정차되고
때론 그 시간에 주차되어
기울어 멈춘 시계추 마냥
네모 세상 빗금 그어진
세모와 세모 마주하며
더 가까이 하기에는 멀어
더 멀찌감치에 머문다

The Paradox of Stillness 고요함의 역설

Sometimes stopped in thought

Sometimes parked in that time

Like a tilted pendulum stopped

Diagonal in a Square World

Triangles and triangles facing each other

It's too far to get closer

It's further away staying.

유리공 카오스 Glass Ball Chaos

이해하고 공감하지만 타협은 할 수 없어
모나지 않았지만 시작과 끝 알 수 없고
영원히 만날 수 없는 폭포와 같아

Glass Ball Chaos 유리공 카오스

I understand and sympathize, but I can't compromise
It's not difficult but, the beginning and the end unknown
It's like a waterfall you can't meet forever.

제**2**부

허상 Delusion

끝없는 신뢰로
내 마음 굳게 두던
찰라의 안락함

어느 날 갑자기
확연해지는 흑빛
빅뱅은 일어나고

끝없이 샘솟는
흐트러진 퇴색빛
그 데칼코마니

아련한 빙하 끝
그마저 생명수로
시공 잊은 그 곳

햇살 가득찬 수중
고결이 지날 때에
소용돌이만 치네

Delusion 허상

With infinite trust
Believed unwavering
In a flash comfort

One day sudden
Blackness becomes clearer
Big bang happens

endlessly springing up
disheveled fading light
That decalcomania

Deep of a glacier,
That is with life water
Forgot the time and space

Under the sunlit waters
When noble waves pass
Only whirlpool surge up

찰라의 양면 The dichotomy of fleeting moments

보석의 길 위에
흔적이 머무나 봐

회향(廻向) 화살표
온전한 다리 같아

잠시 멈추어선
순간들도 흐르고

긴 호흡 추스린
영원 속에 갇히듯

순간 오르내린
그 터도 잊히듯

The dichotomy of fleeting moments 찰라의 양면

On the Path of the Jewel
the traces linger

Arrow mark that send into space
It's like a complete bridge

I stop for a moment
Moments flow by

Long breaths calm down
Like being trapped in eternity

The shiny, then dimmed
and then forgotten...

아름다운 거리 Graceful distance

텅 비어버린 듯한
연의 자락들
그림자 사이에도
거리가 있는 거다

모두 흉터 하나씩
가리워 둔 것은
미지근한 스침마저
아리기 때문이다

Longing 2 그리움2

A single star, a dot, whispered as it swam by.

It was a dot, even in its dazzling garb of light.

because it was too small, too far away to even be seen.

인생이란 Life is.

삶은 자기 상태의 앎이 전부이다
그 어떠함도 자리에 충실했을 뿐
최초로 돌아가는 것이 아니라
새로운 최초를 맞이하는 것일 뿐

Life is. 인생이란

Life is all about knowing your state of being

Nothing has ever been anything but faithful to its place

It's not a return to the beginning

It's just a new beginning.

시작과 소멸 Beginnings and Annihilation

소진 공격의 흑빛 잔재쯤이야
미소라는 날개로 소멸시키고
영롱한 영역 중앙으로 진입해
시작과 끝의 시작이었던 거기
모든 것의 또 다른 시작과 끝일
거기에서 또 다른 태초인 거야

Beginnings and Annihilation 시작과 소멸

In the remnants of the dark hue of relentless attack,

With a smile as wings, it dissolves away,

Entering the center of a resplendent realm.

There, where the beginning and end had their start,

It is another beginning and end of everything,

A place that is yet another genesis.

석고상 Plaster Statue

해오름의 황금빛 숨결
시리게 푸르른 물결에 닿아
해넘이 즈음에 초록빛 너머
달오름과 마주할 거기에
투명한 광채로 서 있는
이전의 나와 이후의 자아
지금의 나와 늘 함께였다고

Plaster Statue 석고상

The golden breath of the sunrise
touches the crisp blue waves.
Beyond the green at sunset
There to face the moonrise
standing in transparent white radiance
My former self and my later self
have always been with me.

삶이라는 시 Sonnet of being

삶은 물결이다
시련과 기쁨으로 흔들리며
가끔은 거칠고 격정적이지만
때로는 부드럽고 온화하다

삶은 불꽃이다
꿈과 열정으로 타오르며
때로는 어둠 밝히지만
때로는 사랑 피워낸다

삶은 여행이다
모험과 발견으로 가득 차며
때로는 어려움 만나지만
때로는 신비 만난다

삶은 노래이다
감동과 울림으로 가득하며
때로는 슬픔 안고 있지만
때로는 희망의 멜로디 부른다

Life is a mystery.

Filled with moments beyond comprehension,

Sometimes posing questions,

But also finding answers.

Life is a beautiful poem

Where each of our joys and sorrows reside

A collection of precious moments,

유리볼의 진실을 찾아서 Seeking Truth Within the Glass Ball

투명한 유리볼 세상
무수한 굴레 속에서
균형의 고지인 그곳
진실을 찾는 여행자

고요로 정화된 마음
시공 초월 존재의 품
머무는 순간이
그때이자 내일이 된

통합된 마음과 육신
모든 존재와 일체
별빛의 발화점들이
무한 사랑빛 도포로

폭풍우 지난 그 자리
순수 회귀된 심장 속
유영하는 고요함
하나된 보석으로
불멸의 실재가 되다

Seeking Truth Within the Glass Ball

유리볼의 진실을 찾아서

In a transparent glass ball world,
Amidst countless constraints,
At the pinnacle of balance,
A traveler seeks the truth...

With a serene and purified mind,
Embraced by the transcendental realm,
In the fleeting moment, this place
Becomes both then and tomorrow...

With a unified mind and body,
In oneness with all existence,
The sparkles of starlight
Envelop the world in infinite love...

In the place where the storm has passed,
Within the pure, regressed heart,
The floating serenity
Becomes a unified jewel,
Becoming an immortal reality⋯

흑백의 옷을 벗고 Black-and-white shredding

무지개 색으로 물들어 피는 시간의 춤
하얀 종이 위에 펼쳐진 새로운 음악

깨달음 얻은 후, 흑백논리 벗어나며
자유로운 상상의 나래 펼치는 시

땅 위에서 떠다니는 구름의 자유
바다속 헤엄치는 물고기의 맑은 미소

숨 쉬듯 자유롭게 피어나는 꽃들
바람과 춤추며 흩날리는 나비의 자유

제한 없는 색채와 환상적인 세계
깨어난 상태에서 노래하는 시의 자유

흑백논리 벗어나 깨닫고
자유로운 상태에서 노래한다

자유로운 색채와 무한한 가능성
꿈꾸는 마음으로 노래하는 시의 자유

Black-and-white shredding 흑백의 옷을 벗고

The dance of time, painted in the colors of the rainbow,
A new melody unfolds on the blank canvas of white paper.

After attaining enlightenment, transcending black-and-white logic,
A poem unfurls the wings of boundless imagination.

The freedom of clouds floating in the sky,
The serene smile of a fish swimming deep in the ocean.

Flowers blooming freely as they breathe,
Butterflies dancing and fluttering with the wind.

Unrestricted hues and a fantastical world,
A poem sings in the awakened state of freedom.

Breaking free from black-and-white reasoning,
In a liberated state, we sing.

The freedom of vibrant colors and infinite possibilities,
A poem sings with a dreaming heart.

아무렇지 않을 용기 The courage to not care

괜찮아, 괜찮지 않아
이 합주는 언제나 끝날까

The courage to not care 아무렇지 않을 용기

It's okay, it's not okay

Will this ensemble ever end

겨울 달의 운명 Fate of the Winter Moon

눈 내리던 겨울밤 투명한 달 떠 오르고
깊은 숲속에서 숨죽인 포효 울리누나

켜켜이 언 눈 쌓인 샛길이 빙하 같아라
이제나 녹으려나 녹기 전 또 얼었더라

소복히 쌓이고 딱딱하게 굳는 하얀 밤
음력 15일 겨울달이 눈부시게 시리더라

세상 만물이 멈칫 허공에 머무르는 모양
그건 생겨나고 상실되는 그 순간

Fate of the Winter Moon 겨울달의 운명

On a winter night when snow was falling,

A transparent moon rose,

And a suppressed roar echoed in the deep forest.

The path covered with piled up snow resembled an icy river,

Will it melt now, but it froze again before it melted.

The white night piled up softly and hardened firmly,

The winter moon on the 15th day of the lunar calendar shone brightly cold.

It seemed as if everything in the world paused in mid-air

That's the moment when it's created and lost

남남은 아무나 되나
(아무도 아닌 사람이 되는 연습)

Practice being nobody

행여나 마주치면
낯선 사람으로
모르는 사람이기를
갈망했는데
본능처럼
바보처럼
나는 부른다

시린 현실은 지나고
이미 투박한 망상만 남은

겨울과 봄 사이의 온도에서 멈춘
사랑과 증오 퍼지는 와이너리에서

Practice being nobody

(아무도 아닌 사람이 되는 연습 : 남남은 아무나 되나)

If a chance encounter

Among the many passersby

As one person

A stranger to a stranger.

But instinctively

Like a fool

They naturally exchange greetings

The harsh reality is gone

Already only delusions remain

Stopped in temperature between winter and spring

In a winery where love and hate spreads

가을비 Autumn Rain

가을비가 내리면

여름별 배웅하려
가을별이 마중 나와

뿌리 깊은 억새풀
진베이지로 물들어

가을별 배웅하고
겨울별 맞이 준비에

그 가을비 내리면

Autumn Rain 가을비

It's raining in the autum

To see off the summer star
The autumn star comes to greet you

and the deep-rooted Silvergrass
have turned dark beige

After seeing off the autumn star
I'm excited to welcome the winter star

If it autum rains like it did then...

맑은 물빛 Clear water color

투명한 맑은 호수에
영롱한 빛들 시기하지 마

작은 잉크 한방울 한방울
호수에 가라앉아 있어

서로 다르기에 흡수할 수 없어
바닥 깊이 더 깊이
숨기고 가라앉힌다고

여기저기 종기처럼
솟아 오르는 트러블 덩이
그것들 앓느라 호수 오염된다고

Clear water color 맑은 물빛

On a crystal clear lake
Don't envy the brilliant lights

Tiny drops of ink
It's sinking in the lake.

Can't absorb them because they're different
Deeper and deeper into the bottom
Hide them and sink them

Like boils here and there
like boils.
Pollute the lake.

다채로움의 노래〈나〉

The Song of Vibrant Colors_Subheading: Me

오로라의 오묘한 영롱함이랄까
무어라 콕 집을 수 없지만
어떤 날은 평온하다가 폭풍우 치고 그랬거든

장미의 가시 닮았다고나 할까
무어라 콕 집을 수 없지만 늘 그래왔어
어떨 때는 뭉툭하다가 뾰족하게 찌르고 그랬지

비포장길 맨발로 걷는 기분이랄까
무어라 콕 집을 수 없지만 늘 그래왔어
이럴 때는 보드랍다가 저럴 땐 거칠기만 했지

벨벳카펫을 밟는 느낌일 거야
무어라 콕 집을 수 없지만 늘 그래왔어
이러함에도 녹아버렸고 저러함에도 포근했었지

청포도의 향기를 품고 있을 거야
무어라 콕 집을 수 없지만 늘 그래왔어
겨울에도 초록빛이었고 봄에도 초록빛이었어

에메랄드 빛깔일 거야
무어라 콕 집을 수 없지만 늘 그래왔어
깊은 바다 동경하고 광활한 우주 사랑하거든

The Song of Vibrant Colors_
Subheading: Me 다채로움의 노래〈나〉

Is it the mysterious brilliance of the Aurora?

I can't pinpoint it, but

Some days it was calm and then it stormed.

Can you say it resembles a rose's thorn?

I can't pinpoint it, but it's always been like that.

Sometimes it's blunt and sometimes it's sharp.

It feels like walking barefoot on a dirt road.

I can't pinpoint it, but it's always been like that.

At times like this, it was soft, but at other times, it was rough.

It'll feel like you're stepping on a velvet carpet.

I can't pinpoint it, but it's always been like that.

I melted despite this and felt cozy despite that.

She'll have the scent of green grapes

I can't pinpoint it, but it's always been like that.

It was green in the winter and green in the spring too.

It will be emerald colored

I can't pinpoint it, but it's always been like that.

I long for the deep sea and love the vast universe.

제 **3** 부

비상 **Fly up**

먹구름 낀 하늘 열린다
인고의 기다림

가슴에 빛 파고든다
영롱한 무지개빛의 때

샛별이 내게 속삭였다
빛가루 쏟아지던 날

Fly up 비상

Dark Skies Open
A long, hard wait,

light penetrates the heart.
A time of brilliant rainbow light,

the stars whispered to me
When the light powder was falling…

순수로의 초대 **A whisper of pure serenity**

신비롭고 영롱한 빛들 중에
가장 빛나던 별의 모든 것이었을
그 고귀함은 깃털처럼 사치스런 자태 아니라
오염되지 않은 그 무엇이었을 뿐더러
가장 맑고 깨끗한 심연의 순수였던 게야

A whisper of pure serenity 순수로의 초대

Among the mysterious and brilliant lights

It was everything about the brightest star

Its nobility is not a luxurious appearance like a feather.

Not only was it something uncontaminated,

It was the clearest and purest purity of the abyss.

나의 다섯 살 여름(여전한 향수)

My Summer at 5 (Nostalgia)

해질녘 붉은 황금빛으로 물들던 서쪽 산자락
소나무 숲속의 바람소리 맞이하는 한여름 정오
태양은 지붕으로 올라가 사방으로 가꾸어진 화단 비춘다

그 빛이 보라색 꽃 비추면 보라빛 태양이 되고
울타리 휘감은 잎사귀 비추면 초록빛 태양이 된다

장독대 옆에 자리 굳힌 핑크빛 철쭉나무 평온한 자태 뽐낸다
이름모를 식물들이 투명한 코팅액 바른 것처럼 광채 뿜으며
철쭉을 경호한다
강렬한 햇볕으로 일광욕 즐기는 된장, 고추장, 간장들이 알
몸으로 구수한 땀내 풍긴다

자그만 텃밭에서 중간 크기 아욱 따서 된장국 끓이고
상추와 풋고추, 부추를 시원한 샘물에 씻어 점심 준비한다
일광욕 즐긴 고추장과 된장 섞어 세계 최고 쌈장으로 탄생시
켜 상추쌈으로 공복 채우는 한낮, 연자줏빛 맨드라미 눈동자
에 들어와 정열을 배운다

한 편의 영화처럼 몇십 년 이상 커왔을
거대한 전나무 그늘에 걸터앉는다
새콤달콤한 매자 열매 디저트 되었던 시절
가슴 쩌릿하게 그리워진다

My Summer at 5 (Nostalgia)

나의 다섯 살 여름(여전한 향수)

The western mountainside dyed red and golden at sunset
Midsummer noon greeting the sound of the wind in the
pine forest
The sun rises to the roof and illuminates the flower beds
planted in all directions.

When that light shines on a purple flower, it becomes a
purple sun.
When the leaves wrapped around the fence shine, they
become a green sun.

The pink azalea tree next to Jangdokdae shows off its
peaceful appearance.
Unknown plants guard the azaleas with a radiance as if
they had been coated with a transparent coating.
Soybean paste, red pepper paste, and soy sauce are bath-
ing in the strong sunlight, naked, giving off the delicious
smell of sweat.

I pick medium-sized mallow from a small garden and make soybean paste soup.

Prepare lunch by washing lettuce, green peppers, and chives in cool spring water.

In the middle of the day, when you fill your empty stomach with lettuce ssam by mixing red pepper paste and soybean paste after enjoying the sun, you learn passion by entering the eyes of a light purple cockscomb.

Like a movie, it has grown over several decades
Sitting in the shade of a huge fir tree
A time when sweet and sour barberry fruit was a dessert. I miss it very much.

여백 **Abyssal Void**

깊은 곳에 고요한 빛이 스미어
멈춘 듯한 세상 사라지는 시간 속
청량한 공기와 풀잎 하나
그득한 조화로 완성되어 가네

순수 뿌리 닮은 공간
그림 된 듯한 세상은 느리게 흐르고
고요한 햇살 포근한 바람되어
온전한 존재로 이끌어 간다

시간과 공간 사이 자유로워져
비추는 빛 무한한 여백 되어
포근한 꽃잎 눈부신 은행잎처럼
무한한 여백과 완전히 하나되어 간다

Abyssal Void 여백

A silent light is absorbed from deep within.
In a world that seems to have stopped, in a time that disappears.
A breath of fresh air and a blade of grass
are completed in harmony.

In this space that resembles pure roots
The sketched world moves slowly
The calm sunshine becomes a warm breeze
Taking you to a complete existence.

Moving freely between time and space
The light that shines becomes an infinite margin.
Like a cozy flower petal, like a dazzling ginkgo leaf.
Becoming fully one with the infinite margin

고요 Calmness

오늘은 새소리 나는 음악 틀어야지
가부좌 틀어 습관처럼 비손하고
눈 감으며 울창한 숲 걷자
숲 정중앙에 도착했을 때
잠들다 깬 나의 목부터
상체의 혈류와 근육들 활력소 느껴야지

누워서 허리와 하체 깨우기 위해
뼈마디 마디에 들어가 호흡하고
자연스레 눈 떠질 때
두발로 땅덩어리 들어 올려야지

두 팔 뻗어 하늘부터 우주 만지고
나를 비추는 별에게 노크하니
오늘도 살아있게 해줄 소원
투명한 잔에 담아 들이킬 거야
오늘도 내일도 우주의 별들 만나야지

Calmness 고요

Today, let's listen to music that sounds like birdsong.
I did our customary cross-legged prayer hands.
and take a walk in the dense forest that I can see when I
close my eyes.
When we reached the middle of the forest
From the neck of my physical body, which has been rest-
ing as if in sleep.
I will feel the blood flow in my upper body and the vigor
of my muscles.

To lie down and awaken my lower back and lower body
and breathe into every bone in my body.
When my eyes naturally open
I'm going to lift off the ground with both feet.

I stretch my arms out and touch the universe in the sky.
I tap the stars that shine on me
A wish that will keep I alive today
I'm going to drink it out of a clear glass.
Today and tomorrow I will meet the stars of the universe
too

영원한 교향곡 0번

펴낸날 2024년 3월 25일
지은이 최경희
기　획 김영일
편　집 선정애 · 김동균
펴낸곳 한국문학세상
　　　　등록번호: 제25100-2015-000088
　　　　주사무소: 서울특별시 동작구 사당로17길 8
　　　　　　　　　 대림프라자 1층 124호
　　　　홈페이지: www.klw.or.kr
　　　　전　　화: 02-6402-2754
　　　　이 메 일: sulmaster@naver.com

인　쇄 ㈜한국학술정보

ISBN 979-11-87445-51-7 (03810)

값 10,000 원